RUMPELSTILTSKIN

by the
Brothers Grimm

Illustrated by
Dennis Hockerman

Troll Associates

Troll Associates, Mahwah, N.J.

Library of Congress Catalog Card Number: 78-18079
ISBN 0-89375-140-5

Once there was a poor miller who had a beautiful daughter. When he met the king for the first time, the miller wanted to make a good impression. He said, "I have a daughter who knows how to spin straw into gold." The king replied, "Then bring her to me, for I want to see this myself!"

When the miller's daughter arrived at the castle, the king took her to a room where there was a spinning wheel and some straw. "Spin this straw into gold," he commanded. "If you value your life, you must do it before dawn." Then he locked the door and left the girl alone.

Of course, the miller's daughter had no idea how to turn straw into gold. So she sat down and began to cry. Suddenly, a little man entered the room. "And why do you weep?" he asked.

"I weep because I must spin this straw into gold," cried the girl. "But I don't know how."

Then the little man asked, "What will you give me if I do it for you?" The girl took the necklace from around her neck and gave it to the dwarf, who immediately sat down at the spinning wheel. *Whirr, whirr, whirr*—the spinning wheel went round and round. By morning, the strange little man had finished. Where the straw had been, there was now a huge pile of spun gold!

When the king returned, he was amazed and delighted. But the sight of all that gold only made him greedy for more. So he led the miller's daughter to another room, which was larger than the first, and was filled with even more straw. "Spin this straw into gold," he commanded. "If you value your life, you must be finished by morning."

When the king had left, the girl again began to weep. Before long, the strange little man appeared. "What will you give me if I spin the straw into gold?" he asked. And the girl replied, "This ring is all I have. But it shall be yours if you help me."

The dwarf put the ring in his pocket and again sat down at the spinning wheel. *Whirr, whirr, whirr*—the wheel went round and round. And by morning, all the straw had been turned to gold.

When the king saw that the second room was now filled with gold, he became even more greedy than before. He took the miller's daughter to the largest room in the palace. Straw was piled from the floor right up to the ceiling. "Spin all this straw into gold," commanded the king. "If you are finished by morning, then you shall be my queen." And as he locked the girl inside the room, the king thought, "She may be only a poor miller's daughter, but what a rich wife she will make."

As on the other nights, the little man appeared and asked, "What will you give me if I help you?" But this time the girl said that she had nothing left to give. "Then you must promise me this," said the dwarf. "If you become queen, you must give me your first-born child."

Now the girl did not know if she would ever be the queen. "Who knows what will come to pass?" she thought. And so she agreed. At once, the little man sat down and began to spin.

In the morning, the king returned. When he saw that the straw had been turned to gold, he was so pleased that he married the girl and made her his queen. Soon, she forgot all about her promise to the strange little man.

A year later, the queen's first child was born. Suddenly, the little man appeared. "It is time for you to keep your promise," he said. The queen was very frightened. She offered him all the riches in the kingdom if only she could keep her baby. But the little man replied, "A child is the greatest treasure in the world, and you have promised yours to me!"

Then the queen began to beg and plead. She cried and she wept. Finally, the little man said, "If you can guess my name before three days pass, then you can keep the child."

That night, the queen thought of all the names she had ever heard. And her messengers went through the kingdom searching for others. In the morning, the little man appeared and asked, "What is my name?" First the queen guessed ordinary names. Then she guessed more unusual ones, like Caspar, Melchior, and Balthazar. And

at each one, the little man jumped gleefully up and down, crying, "No! No! That's not my name!"

On the second day, the queen began guessing strange and curious names, like Cowribs, Spindleshanks, and Spiderlegs. But the little man jumped up and down, crying, "No! No! You'll never guess it!"

When the third day arrived, a messenger came to the queen. "As I was wandering through the woods," he said, "I came upon a little house. A fire was burning near the house. And a strange little man was dancing and hopping around the fire. And as he danced, he sang these words:

Today I bake, tomorrow I clean,
I'm going to take the child from the queen.
A fiddle, a faddle, a needle, a pin,
My name is a secret: it's Rumpelstiltskin!"

When the queen heard this, she was overjoyed. At last she knew his name! Soon, the little man appeared again. "Your three days are up," he said. "Now, what is my name?"

The queen asked, "Is it Tom?"

"No! No!" cried the dwarf, jumping up and down in delight. "That's not my name!"

"Is it Dick?" asked the queen.

The little man danced about and shouted, "No! No! You're wrong again!"

Then the queen asked,
"Is your name Rumpelstiltskin?"

At that, the little man began to scream at the top of his lungs. "A witch told you that! A witch told you that!" He grew so angry that he stomped about the room in a rage. He stamped his right foot down so hard, and it sank so deep that he could not pull it out!

Then he grabbed his left leg with both hands. He pulled so hard that he split himself in two!

And that was the end of Rumpelstiltskin.